THE STORY OF THE EASTER BUNNY

By Sheila Black

Illustrated by Robyn Officer

Produced by Ariel Books

A GOLDEN BOOK • NEW YORK

Western Publishing Company, Inc., Racine, Wisconsin 53404

Chapter One

Early

Once upon a time there was a little rabbit named Early. He lived with his mother, father, and three brothers— Quicksilver, Clover, and Acorn—in a cozy rabbit hole at the top of a grassy hill.

Early had been given his name because he was born just before dawn one Sunday morning. He had been born too early, too. He was a runt, his mother said. One of his paws turned inward just a little, so that instead of hopping straight ahead, he zigzagged from side to side.

He was by far the slowest of his brothers. Quicksilver could run faster than the wind. Clover was strong and could pull carrots out of the ground quicker than the blink of an eye. Acorn, the oldest, was clever. He knew all sorts of useful things, such as where to find lettuce and how to tell which way the wind was blowing.

But Early was just Early. His brothers used to say that he should have been called Late. They said he was not much good at anything. He liked flowers and birds and butterflies. He was best at daydreaming.

As he sat and gazed up at the sky, Early would make up wonderful stories about flowers that danced and talked to each other, and the colors of the rainbow, and where the snowflakes came from.

"I don't know what I will do with you, Early," his father said. "You're a daydreamer." But his mother said Early would be just fine. He was a good-hearted little rabbit, and that was what mattered.

Early liked making up stories, and he liked listening to stories. His aunt Sophia was a famous storyteller. In the evening all the rabbits of the grassy hill used to gather around her. She would tell stories about faraway lands, strange animals, and magic happenings. Early loved all her stories, but his very favorite was the story of the Easter Bunny.

There really was an Easter Bunny. All the young rabbits had heard about him. He was the most famous rabbit of all. Every year on Easter Sunday he traveled the world, bringing eggs to all the children.

Aunt Sophia had actually seen the Easter Bunny once when she was young. Early made her tell about it over and over again.

It had happened just after sunrise one Easter morning. Aunt Sophia had gone out very early, and she had seen him on the horizon. He had been just a flash of white on the hillside, for the Easter Bunny was the fastest rabbit in the world. But she had seen that he was carrying a basket filled with eggs that gleamed like jewels.

One night, when they were all gathered around, Aunt Sophia told the young rabbits something wonderful. When the Easter Bunny grew old and tired, she said, he chose a new Easter Bunny from among the best of all the rabbits in the world.

Quicksilver, Clover, and Acorn lifted their heads proudly. They were surely among the best young rabbits in the world. But Early just looked at the ground. The best? He wasn't the best at anything.

Then Aunt Sophia asked all the young rabbits what they would like to be when they grew up. Quicksilver said he would like to be the fastest. Clover said he would like to be the strongest. Acorn said he wanted to be the cleverest rabbit in the world.

Aunt Sophia nodded.

She turned to Early and asked, "What about you?"

Early's ears turned pink. "I—I would like to be the Easter Bunny," he whispered shyly. He had not meant to say it—it had just popped out.

Everyone laughed. "You!" they cried. "Why, you're the slowest! You're the weakest! The Easter Bunny doesn't just sit on a hillside and look up at the sky. He's the fastest rabbit in the world! You could never be the Easter Bunny."

Early's ears turned an even brighter pink.

The seasons passed. Early grew, but not very much. Everyone agreed that he was rather small for a rabbit who was almost grown up.

Now his brother Quicksilver was almost twice his size and could run across the grassy hill in a flash. Clover was almost three times his size—"as big as a cat," the other rabbits said admiringly. He could pull the largest carrots out of the ground with no trouble at all. As for Acorn, he was so clever that everyone on the hill asked his advice about all sorts of things— how to find the way home in a blizzard or escape from a hunter or a fox.

But people just laughed at Early.

"He's sweet-natured," everyone said, "but with a limp like that—" They shrugged. Early was not much good at anything.

In the mornings he could be seen sitting, watching everything.

In the springtime he looked at the first leaves that appeared on the trees and saw the tiny shoots of grass grow up out of the ground.

In the summer he smelled the heather and watched the sleepy dragonflies gather over the pond at the bottom of the hill.

In the fall he watched the birds fly south and the leaves change from green to red to gold.

He was often lonely, for the other rabbits seemed to be growing up and doing new things. But for Early, nothing changed.

Chapter Two

A Stranger

One December evening, around Christmastime, a group of rabbits huddled under the elm tree. The winter had been worse than usual, and the rabbits had only a few old bits of potato to eat. They were all feeling cold and bad-tempered.

Suddenly Acorn hopped up with a cry. "A stranger is coming up the hill!"

As the stranger came closer they all could see that he was a very old rabbit. He was perfectly white, and his fur shone against the snow with a silver glow.

"Good evening," the stranger said in a deep voice.

The rabbits of the grassy hill looked at him.

"I'm wondering if you could give me a meal and a bed for the night," he said.

Now the rabbits could see that he was shabbily dressed. His blue jacket had seen better days. His ears flopped over, as though he were very, very tired.

"Who are you and where do you come from?" Quicksilver asked rather sternly.

The stranger shrugged. "I'm a stranger," he replied. "I mean no harm, and I've been traveling a long way."

"That's no business of ours," Acorn said in his most grown-up tone of voice. "I'm afraid we cannot help you. We barely have enough food for ourselves."

The other rabbits nodded in agreement.

"And as for a bed," Acorn continued, "why should we take in a stranger who won't even tell us who he is?"

The other rabbits nodded again. They all felt there must be something odd about a stranger who appeared from nowhere. They all moved closer together in their circle, turning their backs on the strange visitor—all of them except Early.

He had been quietly watching the stranger. There was something in the stranger's eyes that made Early want to speak to him. Early had never before seen a rabbit with eyes like that. They were as blue as the sky.

"Excuse me," Early began, hopping forward a step or two.
"We have room in—"

But at that moment Clover reached forward and cuffed
him on the ears, knocking him backward.

"What do you think you're doing?" Acorn whispered crossly.

"Do you always have to be different?" Quicksilver hissed.

And they stepped in front of Early and glared at the stranger,
who turned and hopped away into the icy night.

As soon as the stranger left, it began to snow. The rabbits
gathered together, forming a tight circle against the sharp wind.
The snowflakes fell more and more heavily.

Slowly the rabbits turned and hopped off to
their warm rabbit holes. None of them spared
a thought for the stranger left out alone in
the storm—none of them except Early.

"It's terrible," he murmured to
himself, "for an old rabbit like that to
be outside when it's so cold."

Early peered through the
darkness and the falling snow. He
felt he could not bear to go back
home while the stranger was out all
alone in the storm.

He set off slowly down the hill.
He was going to find the stranger
and bring him home. He didn't care
what the others thought.

The wind whipped the snow into white
clouds around him. The branches of the
trees creaked and groaned. Early struggled
down the hillside.

The woods at the bottom of the hill were silent
except for the moan of the wind. All the animals had
taken shelter from the storm.

Early hopped along as quickly as he could. The snow was
falling so hard that he began to wonder how he would ever find
the stranger.

He kept going. He had never been so far from home before,
not alone. He looked around, but none of the trees looked
familiar. He was sure he was lost in the terrible storm.

He stopped by a fallen tree branch. He was shivering, and his fur was stiff and icy.

"I'll never find the stranger," he murmured to himself. "And how will I ever find my way home?"

Just then, he thought he saw something move across the snow. "Hello!" he cried. "Hello—hello!"

He thought he could hear an answering cry. Then he saw a pair of eyes moving toward him. The eyes drew closer. Early ran forward as fast as he could. It was the old rabbit—the stranger—and he was shaking with cold!

"It's you!" Early cried. "I've been looking for you everywhere."

Early was not certain that he would be able to find his home again. But with the stranger beside him, he just seemed to know the way. They went slowly through the storm to the warmth and safety of Early's rabbit hole.

Early slept near the door and let the stranger have his bed.

When he woke up the next morning, Early ran to his bedroom to see if the stranger was still there, but he had gone. Early asked his brothers about the stranger, but they just stared at him.

"You know he left last night," they told him. "Why would he have come back again?" They did not know that Early had brought the stranger back to the rabbit hole.

Early did not understand why the stranger had left without saying good-bye. Sorrowfully he went back to his room. He pushed open the door.

There, on the freshly made bed, he saw a small package wrapped in brown paper. "To Early," he read on the card, "from a friend."

He tore the paper off the package. Inside was a small egg made of green stone. The color was deep and fresh, like the first spring grass. The green egg glinted in the light.

Early did not want to tell anyone about the stranger's gift. The egg gave him a special feeling that was his alone.

Carefully he wrapped it up again and hid it under his mattress. Sometimes, when no one was around, he would take it out and look at it. It reminded him of spring and summer and days when the world was green and bright.

Chapter Three

 # The Easter Bunny

Winter passed and slowly spring came to the grassy hill. The tips of the trees turned pale green, and the smell of new grass was in the air. Soon after the first flowers bloomed, some exciting news came to the rabbits of the grassy hill.

A messenger, dressed very finely, came and read a proclamation. "The Easter Bunny has decided that he is too old to perform his duties anymore. He is choosing a new Easter Bunny to succeed him."

Quicksilver, Clover, and Acorn could talk of nothing else.

Each morning Quicksilver practiced running. He ran faster and faster until he looked like a flash of light on the hillside. Clover built up his strength until he could turn over big stones with just a single paw. Acorn spoke to all the wise old rabbits. He was trying to improve his knowledge, so that he would be the cleverest young rabbit in the world.

Early, however, just continued to be polite and to offer help wherever it was needed. When his work was done, he sat under the elm tree and made up stories. Sometimes the younger rabbits asked him to tell them his stories, which they loved. And though he was still rather shy, he did.

He hoped that one of his brothers might be the new Easter Bunny. They were so talented, he was sure one of them would be chosen.

March came, then April.

Quicksilver could outrun all the other rabbits, even ones from the next hill. Clover was without question the strongest rabbit around. And everyone agreed that Acorn was awfully clever.

"Any one of them would certainly make a good Easter Bunny!" the rabbits of the hill said proudly.

No one thought of Early.

One morning, toward the end of April, Aunt Sophia cried out
that a procession was coming toward the grassy hill. As all the
rabbits gathered and looked on, a group of finely dressed rabbits
came climbing up the hill. At their head was a very noble rabbit
indeed. The rabbits of the hill whispered to each other that it
could be none other than the Easter Bunny himself. His
silver-white fur gleamed in the sunlight. His waistcoat was the color
of new grass. His jacket was sky blue. In his paw he carried a
silver basket filled with colored eggs of all kinds.

The rabbits of the grassy hill crowded around the visitors.
Quicksilver, Clover, and Acorn were first among them. They
were wearing their finest clothes. Each was secretly sure that he
was the chosen one.

The procession came to a stop. The Easter Bunny stepped
forward.

"I am pleased to say that the new Easter Bunny has been
chosen from among you," he began. "He is the best of all the
rabbits I came across in my journeys. He knows who he is
because I have given him a token of my friendship—an egg
carved out of green stone."

The rabbits looked at each other in confusion. None of them
had ever seen an egg like that. There was a long silence.

At last Early stepped forward shyly. "I beg your pardon, sir. I have a green egg like the one you mentioned. It was a gift from a stranger, but perhaps—perhaps he made a mistake." He took the green egg from his jacket and handed it to the Easter Bunny.

The Easter Bunny clapped him on the shoulder. "Don't you recognize me?" he asked.

And, looking up at his blue eyes, Early saw that the noble rabbit was none other than the stranger he had met that cold winter night so many months ago.

That night the rabbits of the hill celebrated. No one could believe it was Early who was to be the new Easter Bunny. His brothers were sure that somehow a mistake had been made. Only his mother and Aunt Sophia were not surprised.

"I always said you were kindhearted," his mother whispered to him, "and I always said that was more important than anything."

The rabbits of the hillside had danced and eaten into the night. Now they were all tired. Some of them were falling asleep under the stars.

Early was looking up at the sky. He
heard the voice of the Easter Bunny beside
him. "It's time for us to go," he said.

Early turned to look at him. "Are you sure I'm
the one?" he asked quietly. "I can hardly run at all,
you know."

"It doesn't matter," the Easter Bunny answered. "You're the
one."

He reached over and touched Early on the shoulder with his
silver cane. Suddenly Early felt his legs and his paws start to
tingle. He felt as though he could run as fast as anything. He
looked sadly at the grassy hill, but he knew he had to go.

The two rabbits set off together along the hillside. At first
Early was slightly slower than the Easter Bunny. But after a
moment or two, he drew even with him. They ran faster and
faster, until they were no more than a flash of white on
the hillside.

The rabbits of the grassy hill watched them go with a happy
feeling in their hearts.

If one Easter Sunday you see a rabbit carrying a basket full of colored eggs, you will know that he is the Easter Bunny. And although this story took place many years ago, it may well be Early himself. He is much older now, of course, but he is still a daydreamer. And sometimes, when he is tired, one paw turns in just a little bit, just as it used to a long time ago on the green, grassy hill.